I AM READING

BROWN BEAR

GETS IN SHAPE

ALAN DURANT

ILLUSTRATED BY

ANNABEL HUDSON

For Paula, who lit a candle—A. D.
For Simon. x x x—A. H.

KINGFISHER
a Houghton Mifflin Company imprint
222 Berkeley Street
Boston, Massachusetts 02116
www.houghtonmifflinbooks.com

First published by Kingfisher in 2003
This edition published in 2004
2 4 6 8 10 9 7 5 3 1
1TR/0104/TWP/GRS(GRS)/115SEM

LIBRARY OF CONGRESS CATALOGING-IN-PUBLICATION DATA
has been applied for.

ISBN 0-7534-5797-0

Printed in India

Contents

Brown Bear in the Dark

Brown Bear woke with a start.

Crash! Thump!

Something hit the ground so hard

that Brown Bear's house hopped

and wobbled.

Brown Bear sat up in bed.

"Oh!" he cried.

He looked at his clock.

The time was eight o'clock.

It should be light by now,

thought Brown Bear. But it wasn't.

Brown Bear switched on his
bedside light.
He got out of bed and padded
to the window.
He pulled back the curtains,
but all he could see was dark.
His clock said it was morning,
but his window said it was night.

Brown Bear
sat on his bed
and thought.
He thought
about the crash
in the woods.
He thought
about the dark.
He thought
about the time.

Suddenly he *knew* what had happened.
The sun had fallen out of the sky!
"Oh dear, oh dear!" Brown Bear
said to himself.

He thought about
the woods outside
without the sun
in the sky.
It would be dark
and cold—*very* dark and *very* cold.

Brown Bear shivered.

There might be nasty things out there.

There might be horrible witches

with green faces or slimy, slithery

creatures with sharp teeth

or bear-eating monsters . . .

Tramp, tramp, tramp!

Someone was climbing up the stairs.

The monsters were coming to get him!

Brown Bear dived under the bed.

"Go away!" he moaned.

"I don't want to be eaten."

"Brown Bear, it's only me,"

called Bunny.

Bunny lived downstairs.

She was Brown Bear's best friend.

"Did you hear that terrible crash?

What could it be?" said Bunny.

Brown Bear crawled out from

under his bed.

"I know what it was," he said. "Bunny,

the sun has fallen out of the sky!"

He took Bunny to the window and
showed her the dark outside.
"This is awful," said Bunny.
"We should tell Chimp."
Chimp was their friend.
He lived just across the woods.

"Yes," agreed Brown Bear.

He thought for a moment.

"But we'll have to go outside,"
he said unhappily.

"Of course," said Bunny.

"But it's cold and dark, and there
might be nasty things out there,"
said Brown Bear. "There might be
witches or slimy, slithery creatures
or even bear-eating monsters."

Bunny turned pale.

There might be
bunny-eating
monsters out there too,
she thought.

Knock, knock!

Bunny and Brown Bear leaped
and screamed.

Brown Bear dived
under the bed again, and
Bunny hid behind the curtains.

Knock, knock!

There was a monster at the front door!

"There's no one here!"

wailed Brown Bear.

"G-g-g-go a-w-w-way,"

stammered Bunny.

"Brown Bear, open the door!"

called a familiar voice. "It's Chimp!"

Brown Bear got out from under
the bed and crossed the room.
With trembling paws,
he opened the front door.
"Quick, Chimp! I've got
something important to
tell you," Brown Bear gabbled.
He grabbed Chimp and pulled him
inside, slamming the door behind him.
"What is it, Brown Bear?" asked Chimp.
"What's the matter?"
"It's the sun, Chimp," cried Brown Bear.
"It's fallen out of the sky!"
"And the woods are dark and full of
horrible monsters," added Bunny.

Chimp frowned. "I didn't see any horrible monsters," he said.

"And the woods aren't dark. They're bright. The sun is shining. Come and see." Chimp went to the front door and opened it wide. Sunlight spilled in.

Brown Bear blinked and rubbed his eyes.

"Oh," he said.

"Oh," said Bunny.

Brown Bear looked at the window
and pointed.

"But the window's dark," he said.

Chimp led Brown Bear and
Bunny outside. "Look," he said.
A big tree had fallen outside Brown
Bear's window. "That's why it was
so dark in your room."

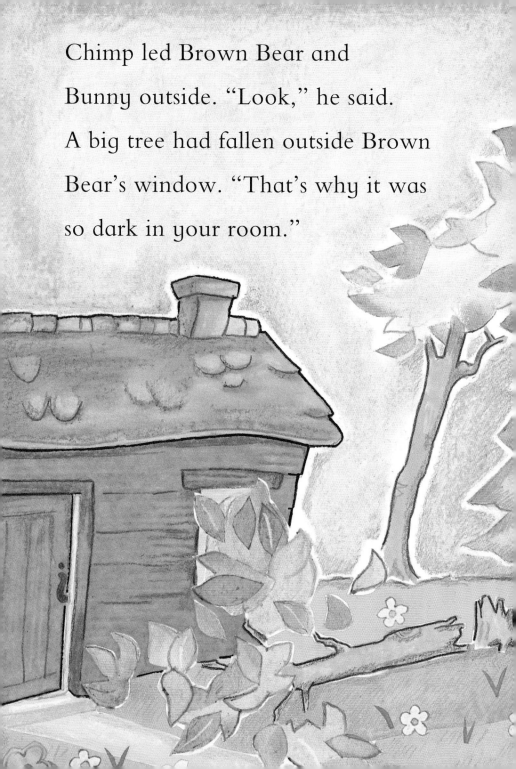

Brown Bear and Bunny
stood in the bright sunlight,
staring at the big tree
and feeling a little silly.

"Well," said Chimp, "I think we should move this tree, don't you?"

"Good idea," Bunny agreed.

"Mmm," said Brown Bear. "But first I think we should go inside and have some breakfast. All this excitement has made me hungry!"

"Now, that," said Chimp with a smile, "is a *very* good idea!"

Brown Bear Gets in Shape

One morning Brown Bear looked

down and got a nasty surprise.

He could not see his feet.

All that he could see was his big,

round tummy.

The more he looked, the bigger and
rounder his tummy seemed to be.
"Oh," said Brown Bear. "Oh dear.
How tubby I have grown."
He went downstairs to see Bunny.

"Hello, Bunny," said Brown Bear.

"Hello, Brown Bear," said Bunny.

Brown Bear looked at Bunny.

Bunny's tummy wasn't tubby.

She could easily see her feet.

"Bunny," said Brown Bear,

"I want to be the same shape as you.

What should I do?"

Bunny thought for a moment.

"What do you eat?" she asked at last.

"Honey," said Brown Bear. "What

do *you* eat?"

"I eat lettuce and carrots," said Bunny.

"Why don't you try eating lettuce and

carrots too?"

So Brown Bear tried lettuce and carrots

. . . for *one whole day.*

He had carrot juice

and lettuce leaves

for breakfast.

He had lettuce
sandwiches and
carrot cake
for lunch.

He had lettuce soup
and carrot sticks
for dinner.

But he didn't like it very much, and he
still couldn't see his feet.

27

When he looked down, his tummy
looked bigger than ever.
"Oh dear, this is no good," he said.
"Maybe Chimp will be able to help."
So Brown Bear went to visit Chimp.
Chimp's tummy wasn't tubby.
He could see his feet.

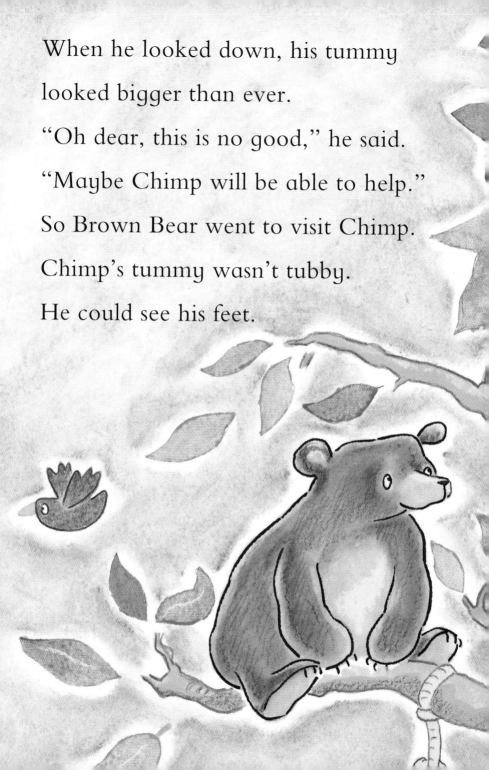

"Chimp," said Brown Bear,
"I wish my tummy was the same
shape as yours. What do you eat?"
"I eat bananas," said Chimp.
"Okay," said Brown Bear. "Then
I will eat bananas too."

Brown Bear ate
bananas for
one whole week.
He ate banana bread

and drank banana
milk shakes.

He even ate
banana peels!

He liked bananas a lot more than lettuce or carrots, but his tummy was still the same shape, and he still couldn't see his feet.

"This is no good," he sighed.

Bunny had another idea.
"Why don't you come for a hop
with me?" she said. "Exercise
is good for getting in shape."
"Okay," said Brown Bear.
So Brown Bear and Bunny
went for a hop through the forest.

Hop,

Hop,

Hop!

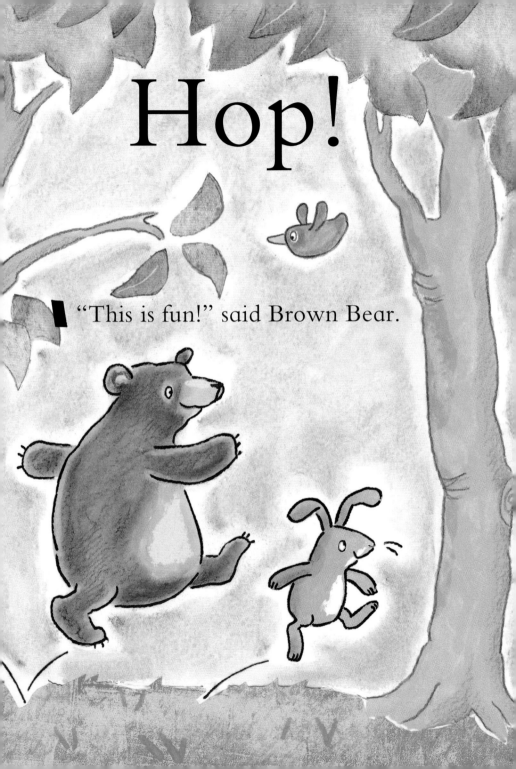

"This is fun!" said Brown Bear.

But then . . .

squelch, squerch, squish!

Brown Bear hopped so hard he was

in mud up to his middle!

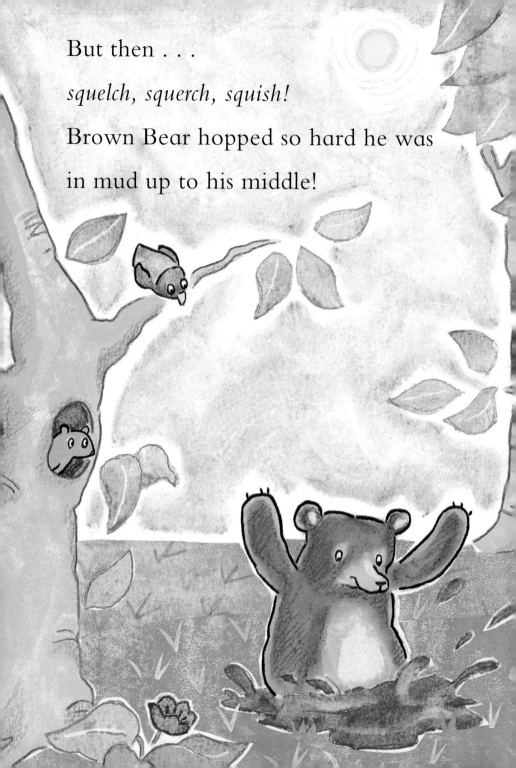

"Help! Help!" cried Brown Bear.
Chimp heard the noise and came out
of his house to help.

Chimp and Bunny pulled Brown Bear
out of the mud.

Then they took him to Chimp's house
and helped him get clean again.
"Why don't we all go to the gym,"
said Chimp.
"That's where I go
to get in shape."

Brown Bear loved the gym.

He leaped on this,

and he pulled on that.

He did sit-ups

and jumping jacks.

Chimp threw a rope to him. "Hey,
Brown Bear, climb up this!" he called.
Brown Bear climbed up the rope.

Then he swung onto another and

another and another.

"This is fun!" cried Brown Bear.

But then *crack! crunch! crash!*

Brown Bear bashed

into the wall,

fell off the rope,

and bumped on his bottom.

"Ow!" howled Brown Bear.

"It's no good," said Brown Bear,

looking down at his tummy.

"My tummy is still round and tubby.

I'll never be able to change my shape."

Bunny looked at Brown Bear. "Brown Bear," she said, "I like your shape. It's, well, bear shaped." "Yes," agreed Chimp. "Bears are *supposed* to have round tummies. Have you ever seen a bear with a flat tummy?"

Brown Bear thought.

He thought very hard.

"Well, no," he said at last.

"I don't think I have."

"You have your shape,

and we have ours,"

said Bunny.

Brown Bear looked

down at his big, round,

bear-shaped tummy.

"Mmm, maybe you're right," he said.

Then he smiled.

"I love my tummy," sighed Brown Bear

happily, and he gave it a little pat.

Then he frowned.

"You don't think it's looking a little flat, do you?" he asked anxiously. "NO!" said Bunny and Chimp together. But Brown Bear went to get some honey . . . just in case.

About the author and illustrator

Alan Durant has written many stories for children of all ages. Most of his books have started life as tales told to his own children. "Brown Bear, Chimp, and Bunny are based on three of my daughter Josie's beanie babies," he says. "She asked me to make up a story about them one evening—and that's how 'Brown Bear Gets in Shape' came about."

Annabel Hudson worked as a lawyer before becoming a full-time illustrator. "Being able to draw and paint all day is brilliant fun," she says. She also enjoys making collages, ripping up bits of paper and sticking them together. Like Brown Bear, Annabel loves honey, "especially toast or crumpets with lots of butter and lots of honey on top."

Strategies for Beginner Readers

Predict
Think about the cover, illustrations, and the title
of the book. What do you think this book will be about?
While you are reading think about what may
happen next and why.

Monitor
As you read ask yourself if what you're
reading makes sense. If it doesn't, reread, look
at the illustrations, or read ahead.

Question
Ask yourself questions about important ideas
in the story such as what the characters might
do or what you might learn.

Phonics
If there is a word that you do not know, look carefully
at the letters, sounds, and word parts that you do know.
Blend the sounds to read the word. Ask yourself if this is
a word you know. Does it make sense in the sentence?

Summarize
Think about the characters, the setting where the
story takes place, and the problem the characters faced
in the story. Tell the important ideas in the beginning,
middle, and end of the story.

Evaluate
Ask yourself questions like: Did you like the story?
Why or why not? How did the author make the story
come alive? How did the author make the story fun to
read? How well did you understand the story? Maybe
you can understand it better if you read it again!